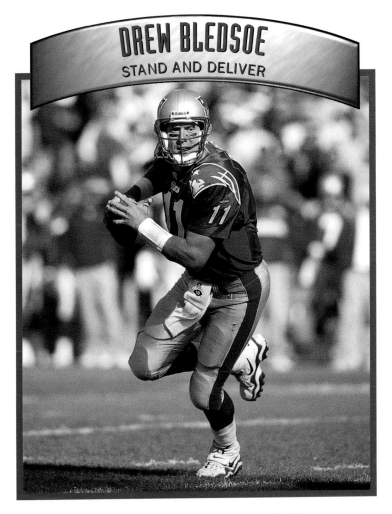

★ SPORTS STARS ★

DREW BLEDSOE
STAND AND DELIVER

BY MARK STEWART

Children's Press®

A Division of Grolier Publishing
New York London Hong Kong Sydney
Danbury, Connecticut

Photo Credits
Photographs ©: Allsport USA: 26, 35 (Al Bello), 17, 44 left (Otto Greule Jr.), 6 (Tom Hauck), 47 (Bill Hickey), 43 (Harry How), 40, 45 left (Jamie Squire), 22 (Damian Strohmeyer); AP/Wide World Photos: 31 (Eric Draper), 30, 32, 45 right (John Gaps III), 21 (Charles Krupa), 34 (Stephan Savoia); Icon Sports Media: 25 (Patrick Murphy-Racey); SportsChrome East/West: 39 (John Williamson), cover, 3, 44 right (Steve Woltmann), 46 (Ron Wyatt); Walla Walla Union Bulletin: 12, 13 (Greg Lehman); Washington State University Libraries: 15, 18 (Historical Photograph Collection).

Acknowledgments: *The author would like to thank Mike Kennedy, who did the research for this book.*

Visit Children's Press® on the Internet at:
http://publishing.grolier.com

Library of Congress Cataloging-in-Publication Data

Stewart, Mark.
　　Drew Bledsoe : stand and deliver / by Mark Stewart.
　　　p. cm. — (Sports stars)
　　　Summary: A biography of the New England Patriots quarterback who led the team to the Superbowl in 1997.
　　　ISBN 0-516-22047-0 (lib. bdg.)　　　0-516-27072-9 (pbk.)
　　　1. Bledsoe, Drew, 1972—-Juvenile literature. 2. Football players—United States—Biography—Juvenile literature. [1. Bledsoe, Drew, 1972- 2. Football players.] I. Title. II. Series.
GV939.B56 S84 2000
796.332'092—dc21
[B]

00-026711

☆ CONTENTS ☆

DO IT, DREW!

Drew Bledsoe takes the snap from center and begins scanning the field for receivers as he backpedals into the pocket. Option one, no good. Option two, no good. Option three, no good. The pass coverage is perfect and his blocking is beginning to break down. He turns to his left to look for the running back who is supposed to be his "safety valve" on this play, but he is nowhere to be found.

Drew is in trouble. Sensing a menacing presence on his blind side, he steps forward quickly and ducks. A gigantic forearm grazes the number 11 on his back as a huge defensive end barrels past. Then Drew spots a receiver coming back toward him. He also sees two defensive backs converging on his teammate.

Drew straightens up, cocks his arm, takes a short stride, and then zings the ball 20 yards on a line to his man. The ball hums through the air, between the lunging defenders—right into the receiver's hands. A moment after Drew releases the ball, he finds himself facedown on the turf, with an angry 330-pound lineman sitting on his helmet. The crowd's reaction is the only way Drew knows his pass has found its target.

It may sound crazy, but this is the life Drew has wanted since he was a little boy. Every time he completes a pass, every time he gets tackled, every time he sits in front of his locker and pulls the uniform off his aching body, he is living his dream.

⋆ 2 ⋆

ALWAYS ON THE MOVE

Someone once said that you can take a boy out of a small town, but you cannot take the small town out of the boy. Drew Bledsoe would be the first to admit that this describes him perfectly. He would also tell you that—football or no football—he is proud of who he is and where he came from.

For this, he gives credit to his parents, Mac and Barbara. They encouraged Drew to excel in sports, but they also pushed him to discover as much as he could about himself and the world around him. "I know I don't have to play football to gain the acceptance of anyone or to prove I'm a good person," Drew says.

Drew was born in 1972, in the town of Ellensburg, Washington. He did not remain there long, however. Mac Bledsoe, a former college football star, decided that being a high school coach made him happy. Drew's family moved all over the state of Washington during the 1970s and early 1980s, as Mac went from school to school. Drew and his little brother, Adam, became quite good at making new friends. And when they had no one to hang around with, they were happy to play with each other.

By the time Drew entered the sixth grade, the family had already changed addresses five times. Wherever they went, however, the Bledsoes could be certain of one thing: Drew would join a school team, and he would be one of its best players. His excellent endurance helped him in running, swimming, cycling, and basketball.

Drew also was an accomplished quarterback. None of the towns he lived in had organized youth-league football, so he played during recess at school. When he heaved the ball to his friends during their games, he imagined himself playing in the Super Bowl like his hero, Terry Bradshaw of the Pittsburgh Steelers.

Mac and Drew spent hours playing catch and discussing the finer points of offense and defense. Mac ran a football camp during the summers, and Drew attended these camps from the time he was a toddler. "It's a real advantage," Drew says of his early exposure to the sport. "You learn football the way a normal kid learns language. I've known 'cover-two' and 'cover-three' since I was in third grade. I learned where the strong safety should be about the time most kids are learning to use a fork."

After years of moving his family around, Mac Bledsoe decided it was time to put down roots in Walla Walla, and that is where Drew got his first taste of organized football. He tried out for the Pioneer Junior High School football team in 1983 and was told, to his amazement, that he was not

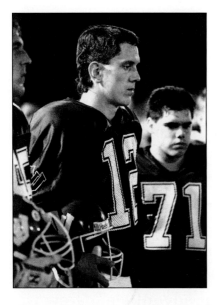

Drew gets ready to start a high-school game. An injury in his first varsity game nearly ended his career.

good enough to start. Thanks to a sudden growth spurt, Drew was now six feet tall—and all arms and legs. His dad says he looked like a praying mantis! It took Drew three years to grow into his body and get his coordination back.

In the ninth and tenth grades, Drew played for Walla Walla High School's junior varsity. Midway through his sophomore year, he was invited to join the varsity team. Drew's dad, who coached the team, did not put him in right away because he was afraid people would think he was favoring his son. He didn't give his boy a chance to start until his fellow coaches urged him to let Drew play.

In Drew's first varsity game, a tackler hit him in the stomach with his helmet. He finished the game, but his stomach still hurt hours later. The Bledsoes took their son to the hospital, where doctors discovered that his liver had been smashed against his spine and was dangerously swollen. Drew had to wait nearly a year before he could play football again.

Drew and his coach talk strategy during a timeout. Drew set a state record for passing yards in a game in his senior season.

As a junior, Drew grabbed hold of the starting job and never let it go. He threw for more than 1,600 yards and 13 touchdowns during the fall of 1988, and was named second-team All-Conference. The following season, he topped 2,500 yards and tossed 25 scoring passes. In one game, he threw for 509 yards to establish a new state record.

College scouts packed the stands for each of Walla Walla's 1989 games. National sports magazines listed Drew among the best prospects in the United States. All of this could have gone to a young man's head, but not Drew's. The moment he walked in his front door, he was just "Biggie," the chubby little kid who used to play in the toilet. "My parents always made it clear that what I accomplished on the playing field had nothing to do with who I was as a person," he says.

After his final high-school football season, Drew had to decide where he would go to college.

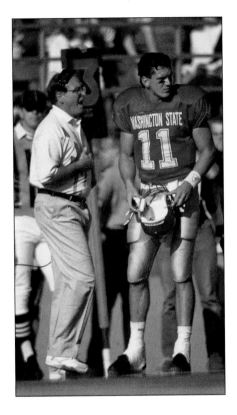

Drew watches a play with Washington State University coach Mike Price.

Everyone assumed Drew would go to the University of Washington because its football team was far superior to Washington State University's (WSU), but WSU had other advantages. It was close to Walla Walla, and the campus in Pullman was small and friendly. WSU's coach, Mike Price, promised Drew he would get a chance to start his very first year. In the end, Drew surprised his dad and all the experts by accepting Washington State's offer.

★ 3 ★

KILLER COUGAR

As promised, Drew got his chance to lead the Cougars in his freshman year. Six games into the 1990 season, Coach Price gave his 18-year-old star the starting job. Many of the team's fans did not like Price's decision, and they let Drew hear it during games. Worse yet, most of the players on the team did not think Drew should be playing. "That year was a zoo," Drew recalls. "It was ugly. There were three separate cliques on the team, and the ones that weren't for me wouldn't talk to me."

A year later, however, Drew was the most popular guy in the Cougars' locker room. By

Drew pitches the ball to a runner during a game against Stanford. After a tough freshman year, he became the Cougars' leader.

not giving up and by showing a willingness to work with those who had opposed him, Drew won over his teammates. Of course, it didn't hurt that he put up the fourth-best passing statistics in school history.

Drew's third college season was one for the books. Everything came together during his junior year. He picked apart defenses at will,

Drew looks the part of a dashing college football star. He was voted All-PAC 10 after his junior year.

and the Cougars rolled over one opponent after another. No longer a laughingstock, WSU was suddenly a Top 20 team.

Drew had three great games that year. Against Montana, he set a school record with 413 passing yards. Against archrival Washington, Drew led his team to an upset in a driving snowstorm. And in the season finale, he squeezed out a 31–28 victory in the Copper Bowl against Utah with an amazing 476 passing yards.

In one season, Drew had developed into a big-time passer. He had the arm, the head, and the heart that pro scouts look for. Convinced he could accomplish no more in the college game, Drew decided to leave Washington State a year early and enter the NFL draft. "I'm not saying college football became too easy for me," explains Drew. "But I felt it was time for a new challenge."

Drew had the full support of his coaches, his parents, and of his girlfriend, Maura. The two had met earlier in the year on the tennis court. Maura did not know Drew was the "big man on campus," and proceeded to destroy him in their singles tennis match. "I asked for a rematch and soon we were dating," Drew remembers. "We've been together ever since."

★ 4 ★

PICK OF THE PATS

Some scouts felt Drew was too easygoing to survive in the NFL. Would he bounce back quickly if things didn't go well? One coach who believed in Drew was Bill Parcells. He had just taken over the New England Patriots, a near-dead franchise in need of leadership. Parcells saw in Drew what he had seen in a soft-spoken, country-boy quarterback named Phil Simms more than a decade earlier: immense talent and intelligence, a willingness to learn, and the toughness to withstand harsh criticism. Parcells and Simms had turned the near-dead New York Giants into a Super Bowl team. Parcells believed he and Drew could accomplish the same thing

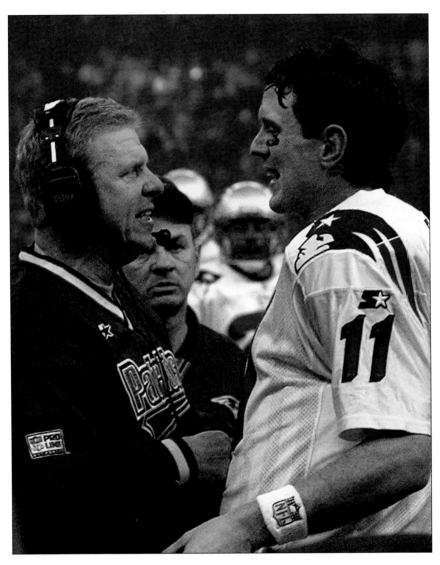

Bill Parcells gives Drew a few words of wisdom. In 1993, he made Drew the NFL's top draft choice and New England's starting quarterback.

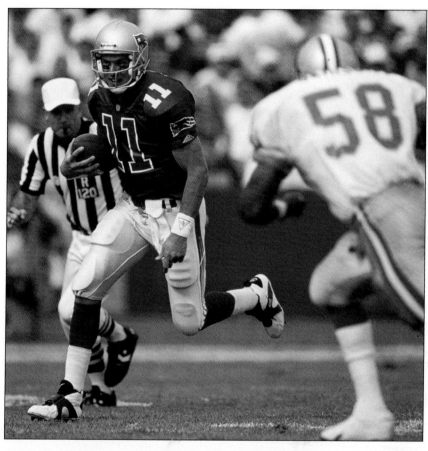

Drew looks for an opening against the Lions in his second pro game. At 21, he was the youngest player in team history.

On opening day in 1993, Parcells made Drew starting quarterback. Although the Patriots lost their first four games, Drew did not feel lost as quarterback. Most of the defenses he saw were familiar to him. He just needed to read and react to them faster. His teammates were young and inexperienced too, but just as talented.

By the middle of the season, everyone was working together and New England was competitive in every game it played. The Patriots finished well, scoring victories over the Bengals, Browns, Colts, and Dolphins in the final four weeks. Despite missing several games with a sore knee, Drew finished the year with 2,494 passing yards and 15 touchdowns (TDs).

Believing that it was foolish to hold Drew back, Coach Parcells went into the 1994 season with a bold plan. He decided to let his second-year star challenge opponents with a high-powered passing attack. At first, the plan looked like a disaster. The Patriots lost six of their first nine games, and most of those losses were due to Drew trying to do too much. In the team's three wins, however, Drew played like an All-Pro. Parcells believed Drew was right on the verge of something special.

In the season's next game, the Patriots promptly fell behind the Minnesota Vikings by 20 points. In the second half, Drew finally rose to the challenge. He threw the ball like no one ever had before, and led the drive that tied the game with seconds left. In overtime, he threw Kevin Turner a lovely 14-yard touchdown pass for a 26–20 win. When the smoke cleared on this fabulous day, Drew owned the all-time records for most passes completed (45) and most passes attempted (70) in a game. Incredibly, not one ball he threw was intercepted!

Drew never cooled off after that. He led New England to six more victories to finish the year at 10–6. He led the league with 400 completions— which was just four short of the NFL record—

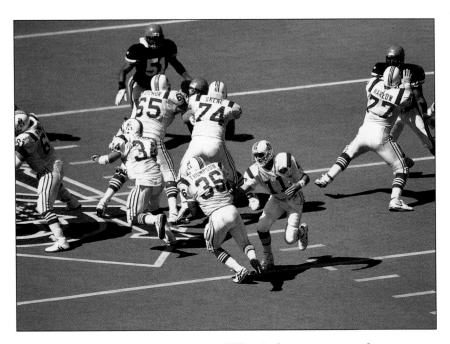

Running a pro offense can be difficult for a young player, but Drew had been executing plays like this since he was a little boy.

and 4,555 passing yards. In the process, he established a new all-time mark with 691 pass attempts. Although the Browns beat the Patriots in the playoffs, the 1994 season was, by any measure, a spectacular success. "We all felt the team was going in the right direction," Drew remembers.

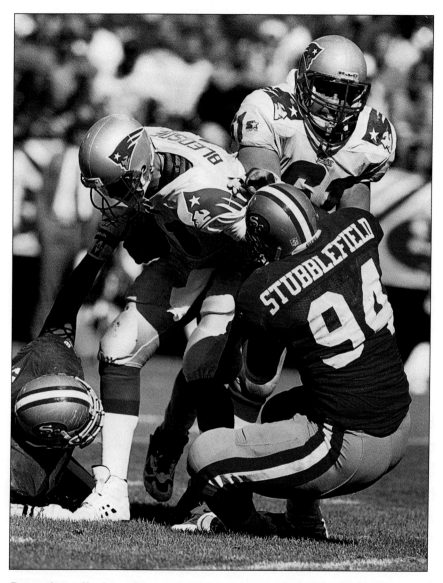

Drew is pulled to the ground by All-Pro Dana Stubblefield of the 49ers. He hurt his shoulder in this game, ruining a promising season.

★ 5 ★

COMING TOGETHER

In 1995, Drew learned that going in the right direction does not guarantee you will get where you want to go—the team fell short of its goals and missed the playoffs. In the season's third week, Ken Norton of the San Francisco 49ers nailed Drew and separated his non-throwing shoulder. A team doctor popped it back in and Drew returned to the game, but he had to sit out the next game because of the pain. From there, the season unraveled. The Patriots finished 6–10.

The lone bright spot for the Patriots was rookie runner Curtis Martin. Opponents were trying so hard to get to Drew that Martin often took the ball and slipped right past the pass-rushers for big gains. He ended up leading the American Football Conference (AFC) with 1,487 yards.

In 1996, the Patriots gave Drew a pair of big-play receivers by acquiring Shawn Jefferson from the San Diego Chargers and drafting Ohio State star Terry Glenn. They also made better use of Curtis Martin's running skills. The Patriots finished first in the AFC's Eastern Division with an 11–6 record. Drew was superb, completing nearly 60 percent of his passes. He threw just 15 interceptions in 623 attempts, and connected for 27 touchdowns.

In the playoffs, Drew guided the team to a win against the Pittsburgh Steelers. Throwing just enough to keep the Pittsburgh defense off-balance, he engineered a pair of first-quarter touchdowns to build a 14–0 lead. When Martin broke off a 78-yard touchdown run in the second quarter, the game was decided. The final score was 28–3. "It was extra special for me," says Drew of his first playoff win, "because dad was on the sidelines that day."

In the AFC Championship, the Patriots faced the Jacksonville Jaguars. The New England defense really came through, giving Drew great field position three times. He converted these opportunities into 17 points, while the defense limited Jacksonville to a pair of field goals in a decisive 20–6 victory. Drew and the Patriots were headed to the Super Bowl!

Against the Green Bay Packers in Super Bowl XXXI, the Patriots looked like losers right from the beginning. On Green Bay's second play of the game, quarterback Brett Favre hit receiver Andre Rison with a great pass, and he scored a 54-yard touchdown. The Packers added a field goal to build a 10–0 lead. Suddenly, the game was looking like a blowout.

Drew celebrates a Super Bowl touchdown against the Green Bay Packers. He threw for 253 yards in the game.

Drew, now a veteran leader, stepped in and brought things back under control. He hit running back Keith Byars for a touchdown to cut Green Bay's lead to 10–7. Drew threw for another touchdown that gave New England a 14–10 lead. Unfortunately, the Patriots' defense gave up 17 points before halftime.

★ ★ ★

In the third quarter, Drew led his team to a touchdown that made the score 27–21. The Patriots' offense jogged confidently to the sideline—they had regained the momentum. Then the unthinkable happened. Desmond Howard fielded the ensuing kickoff a yard from his own goal line and then blew past all 11 Patriots for a heartbreaking 99-yard touchdown. The Patriots never recovered, and the game ended 35–21 after a scoreless fourth quarter.

Drew "threads the needle" against the Packers. He completed 25 passes, but was intercepted four times.

"I'm proud we fought back," says Drew, who
adds that nothing feels worse than losing a
Super Bowl. "You win a bunch of games to get
you there, and you forget what it's like to lose.
To go that far and play that well, and not win,
is hard to swallow."

**Drew congratulates fellow quarterback Brett Favre of the
Packers after Green Bay's 35–21 victory in Super Bowl XXXI.**

★ 6 ★

LIFE WITHOUT BILL

At the age of 25, with a slew of passing records and a Super Bowl already under his belt, Drew Bledsoe seemed to have it all. Everyone agreed he would only get better, and the Patriots were a young team that would improve. Another trip to the Super Bowl seemed just around the corner.

The team's owner, Robert Kraft, thought some changes had to be made in order for his team to return to the big game. He did not like that Bill Parcells had so much power. So the two men parted ways before the 1997 season, with Parcells moving to the New York Jets and former Jets' coach Pete Carroll coming in as New England's new leader.

Patriots' coach Pete Carroll (left) gave Drew a greater leadership role in 1997.

Carroll was a different type of coach. He did not believe in screaming at his players and pushing them past their limits. He believed that sometimes a coach needed to step aside and allow the team's leaders to take control.

Drew welcomed this change. Late in the season, when Curtis Martin went down with an injury, Drew came through with some big plays and produced three straight victories. This enabled New England to become AFC Eastern Division champion again. In the playoffs, however, Drew could do little without Martin's running and the Patriots lost in the second round.

The 1998 season established Drew as one of football's most important players. Working again without Martin, who had signed a free-agent deal

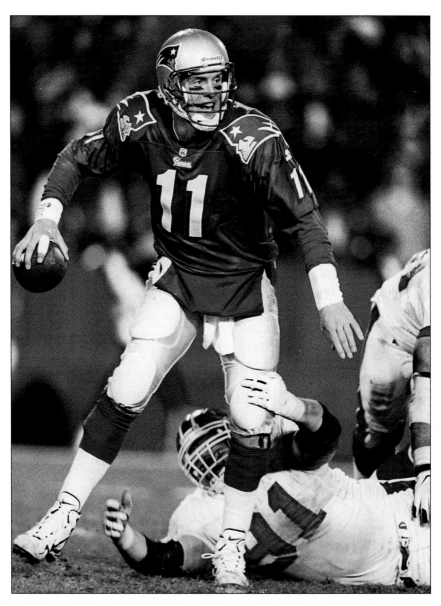

**Drew fights his way out of a sack. He played through the
pain of a broken finger for much of the 1998 season.**

with the Jets, Drew battled to keep the team above .500. In a crucial November game against the Dolphins, he shattered the index finger on his throwing hand, but refused to leave the field. Playing through the pain, he led the team to a 26–23 victory with 423 passing yards and a pair of touchdowns. It was an unforgettable, gutsy performance.

Worried that the team would not make the playoffs if he did not play, Drew continued well into December. Wincing every time he touched the ball, Drew nonetheless helped New England reach the playoffs again. Unfortunately, his finger got worse, and he could not grip the football well enough to take part in the post-season. Drew watched in frustration as the Jaguars beat New England, 25–10.

★ 7 ★

WHAT MATTERS MOST

Drew was beginning to realize that getting back to the Super Bowl takes more than a good team with a good quarterback. A lot of other things have to go right too. Chemistry between the players must be there, and the coaches need to make the right decisions in crucial situations.

In 1999, the Patriots looked good early in the season. New England won its first four games, including thrilling victories over the Jets and Colts. At the season's halfway mark, the team's record was 6–2 and Drew had already thrown 13 touchdown passes.

★ ★ ★

The Patriots were not as good as their
record, however. Even a great player like
Drew cannot carry a so-so team on his back
for long. Opponents realized that Drew was
the Patriots' lone weapon, so they targeted
him. The coaching staff, which was fired after
the season, was unable to give Drew effective
new plays. Frustrated, he began to throw the
ball earlier and earlier, and tried to force
passes into spaces where they just would
not go. The offense stalled and New England
collapsed, winning just two more games. Drew
was bitterly disappointed. "Unfortunately,"
he frowns, "the only thing that we showed
is that we're not a good team."

[right] Drew absorbs a hit after releasing the ball. Opponents
put a lot of pressure on Drew in 1999, when he was New
England's lone weapon.

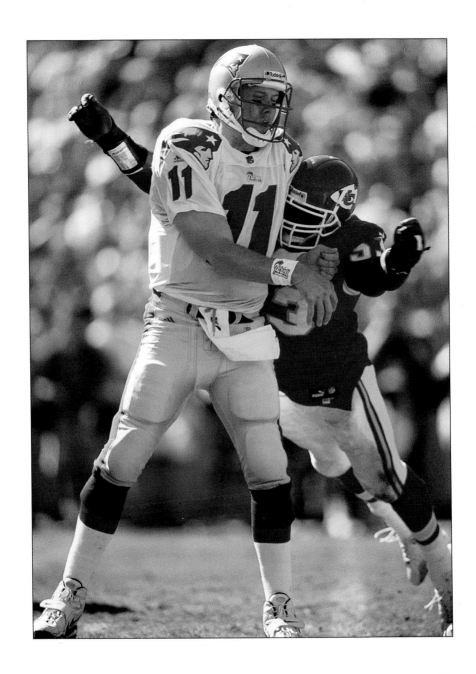

Drew has his sights set on a return to the playoffs. He now knows what it will take to reach the Super Bowl again.

As the holidays ended and the millennium passed—and the playoffs went on without him for the first time in four years—Drew began to think about what he had accomplished in his life, and what was really important. His two young sons, Stuart and John, are important. And the lessons his parents taught him are more important now than ever.

Drew had learned that being a Super Bowl quarterback means knowing how to win. Now he was beginning to see that being a super person means knowing how to deal with losing. Drew decided to use the disappointments of 1999 as building blocks for success in the future.

It was a good decision. As any coach in the NFL will tell you, a great player has to taste defeat before he can truly relish victory. And ultimately, he must understand how football fits into his life. Sadly, most players do not figure this out until their careers are over—when the crowds no longer roar and the big paychecks have stopped.

Drew, however, seems to get it already. "I don't need the fame and fortune," he insists. "Football is not my whole life. There are a lot of other things I enjoy outside football. There are a lot of things more important to me than football. If I didn't have all this stuff, it would have no bearing on what kind of person I am."

For Drew, the fans always come first. He is one of the few NFL quarterbacks who signs autographs for free.

C ★ H ★ R ★ O ★ N

1972 • February 14: Drew is born on Valentine's Day in Ellensburg, Washington.

1983 • The Bledsoe family settles in Walla Walla, Washington.

1987 • Drew plays his first varsity football game.

1989 • Drew becomes one of the best high-school quarterbacks in the region.

1990 • Drew becomes starting quarterback at Washington State University in his freshman year.

O ★ L ★ O ★ G ★ Y

1992 • Drew leads Washington State to an upset victory over the rival University of Washington.

1993 • Drew is the first pick in the NFL Draft and the opening-day quarterback for the New England Patriots.

1994 • Drew sets an NFL record with 691 pass attempts and leads the league with 4,555 passing yards.

1996 • Drew completes 373 passes—the most in the league.

1997 • Drew leads the Patriots to Super Bowl XXXI and earns his third trip to the Pro Bowl.

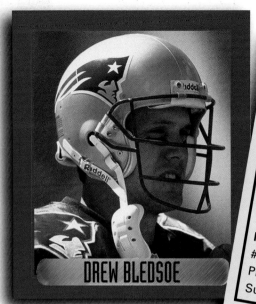

DREW BLEDSOE

DREW BLEDSOE

Place of Birth **Ellensburg, Washington**

Date of Birth **February 14, 1972**

Height **6′ 5″**

Weight **230 pounds**

College **Washington State University**

NFL Records **Most passes in a season; Most passes in a game; Most completions in a game**

#1 in NFL Draft **1993**

Pro Bowl **1994, 1996, 1997**

Super Bowl **1997**

⭐ MAJOR LEAGUE STATISTICS ⭐					
Season	Team	Completions	%	Yards	TDs
1993	Patriots	214	49.9	2,494	15
1994	Patriots	400*	57.9	4,555*	25
1995	Patriots	323	50.8	3,507	13
1996	Patriots	373*	59.9	4,086	27
1997	Patriots	314	60.2	3,706	28
1998	Patriots	263	54.7	3,633	20
1999	Patriots	305	56.6	3,985	19
Totals		2,192	55.9	25,966	147

*Led NFL

ABOUT THE AUTHOR

Mark Stewart has written hundreds of features and more than fifty books about sports for young readers. A nationally syndicated columnist ("Mark My Words"), he lives and works in New Jersey. For Children's Press, Stewart is the author of more than twenty books in the Sports Stars series, including biographies of other football greats Brett Favre and Kordell Stewart. He is also the author of the Watts History of Sports, a six-volume history of auto racing, baseball, basketball, football, hockey, and soccer.